THE
CONJURE WOMAN

THE
CONJURE WOMAN

by WILLIAM MILLER

illustrated by TEREA D. SHAFFER

ATHENEUM BOOKS FOR YOUNG READERS

Atheneum Books for Young Readers
An imprint of Simon & Schuster Children's Publishing Division
1230 Avenue of the Americas
New York, New York 10020

Book design by Becky Terhune
The text of this book is set in Bernhard Modern
The illustrations are rendered in watercolor

Manufactured in the United States of America

First edition
10 9 8 7 6 5 4 3 2 1

ISBN 0-689-31962-2
Library of Congress Catalog Card Number 95-78079

For Liz Szabla, with gratitude and praise   —W. M.

To Aunt Faye and SYBS for all your encouragement   —T. D. S.

Madame Zina, the conjure woman,
lived alone in the woods.
Her house had no windows,
and the door was always shut.

Gourds and other vines
hung down from her roof.
A crow made its nest
in her chimney.

Some people feared Madame Zina.
They said she made the moon
burn red,

killed stray calves,
turned the river into salt.

But when a child was sick—
when the doctor and the preacher
had no answers—the worried parents
turned to Madame Zina.

One night, a boy named Toby burned
with fever. His body ached, and all
he wanted to do was sleep.

His mother and father carried him
from their cabin,
through the freezing night woods,
all the way to the conjure woman's house.

Madame Zina took the boy into her arms
and closed the door.

Around his neck she tied
a bag of herbs.

Around them both she drew
a circle.

And then she sang a song,
strange words, soft music,
into his ear.

Together, they flew
through the night—

above the winter fields,

across the dark ocean,
to their African homeland.

In a village beside a stream,
Toby met his ancestors.

There were chiefs and princesses,
wise men and beggars,
children hiding behind
their mothers' skirts.

They opened their arms
to welcome him,
made a bed for him
beside the roaring fire.

Then the old ones formed
a circle around his bed,
and prayed in voices that
rang through the night.

A tall man brushed his face
with a bright green feather,

another cooled his skin with oil
from a coconut.

A girl, no bigger than Toby,
gave him a cup of strong, black tea.

It tasted of sweet-gum and pepper,
roots that grew in the wild forest.

At last,
the conjure woman
knelt beside his bed,
blew a handful
of dust,
red and gold,
into his eyes.

Toby looked around the circle,
saw himself reflected in the
eyes of all his people.

He felt strong again,
strong enough
to get up from his bed,
touch the faces of the
ones who healed him.

Toby held tight and waved good-bye,
as he and the conjure woman
rose above the fire.

Once more they crossed the dark ocean,
flew above the winter fields

Once more they stood in the circle
drawn by the conjure woman....

Madame Zina opened
the door of her house.

His parents took the boy
from her arms, kissed
his smiling face.

Toby tried to tell them about his journey,
about the ocean and the village,
the old ones who healed him.

But they didn't hear.
They were only glad to have him back,
safe and well again.

Madame Zina, the conjure woman,
blessed the little family
and left them to their joy.